to:

love:

To B.B. Hobbs,
my first grandchild!
I loved you by heart even
before I met you.

♥ PHR

Copyright © 2021 by Peter H. Reynolds

All rights reserved. Published by Orchard Books, an imprint of Scholastic Inc., *Publishers since 1920*. ORCHARD BOOKS and design are registered trademarks of Watts Publishing Group, Ltd., used under license. SCHOLASTIC and associated logos are trademarks and/or registered trademarks of Scholastic Inc.

The publisher does not have any control over and does not assume any responsibility for author or third-party websites or their content.

No part of this publication may be reproduced, stored in a retrieval system, or transmitted in any form or by any means, electronic, mechanical, photocopying, recording, or otherwise, without written permission of the publisher. For information regarding permission, write to Scholastic Inc., Attention: Permissions Department, 557 Broadway, New York, NY 10012.

This book is a work of fiction. Names, characters, places, and incidents are either the product of the author's imagination or are used fictitiously, and any resemblance to actual persons, living or dead, business establishments, events, or locales is entirely coincidental.

Library of Congress Cataloging-in-Publication Data Available

ISBN 978-1-338-78363-6

10 9 8 7 6 5 4 3 2 1   21 22 23 24 25

Printed in China   62

First edition, December 2021

The text type and display are hand-lettered by Peter H. Reynolds.

Reynolds Studio assistance by Julia Anne Young

Book design by Patti Ann Harris and Doan Buu

Peter H. Reynolds

Love You by Heart

ORCHARD BOOKS
An Imprint of Scholastic Inc.

I loved you by heart
even before I met you.
I've loved you always.
I've *always* loved you.

I love every morsel of your being.

I love every smile, every blink.
I love you by heart.
I love your toes, your head, your nose.
I love you by heart.

"I LOVE YOU, LOVE YOU, LOVE LOVE LOVE YOU!"
Plays over and over in my head.

You ARE my song.

I love everything about you.
I love all your ways.
I love ALL your days.
Your good days.

Your blue days.

Your funny days.

Your grumpy days.

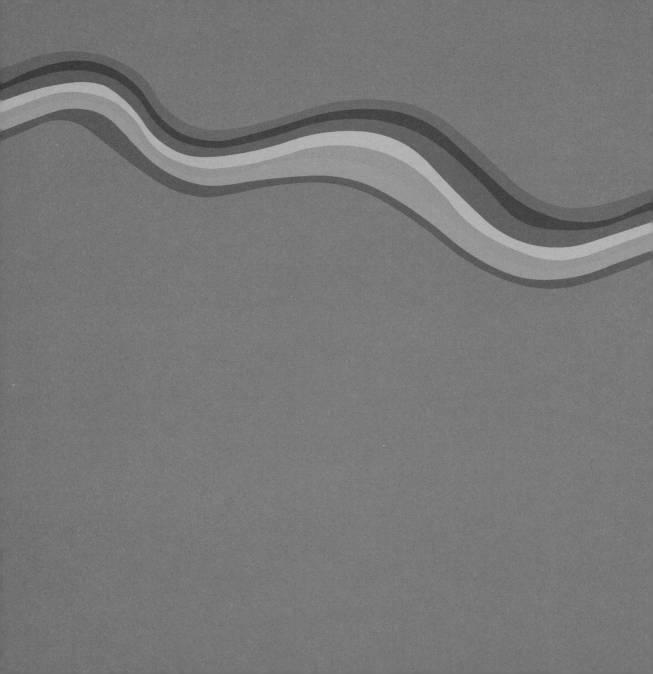

Your rainbow days.
I love everything about you.

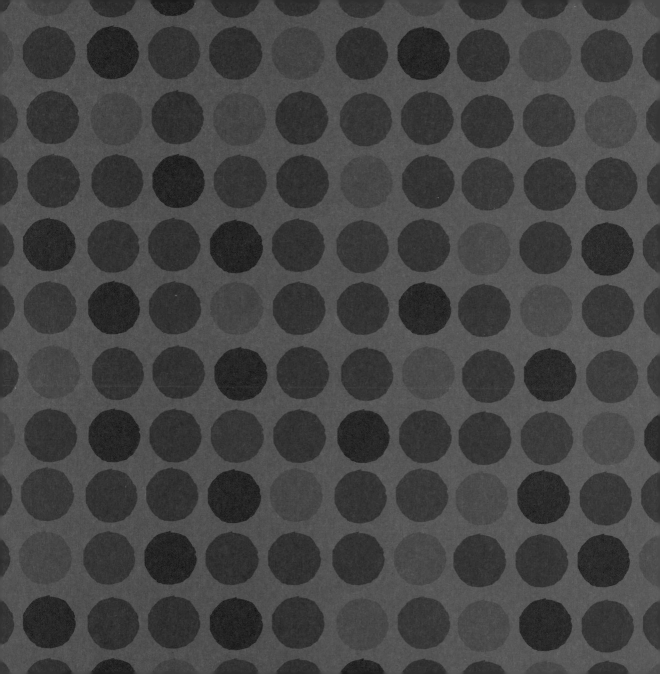

I love how you make me smile,
make me laugh,
make me swoon.

I love you by heart.

I love everything about you.
Your triumphs and joys.
Fumbles and falls.
I'll take it all!

I love you in the morning.
I love you all day.
I love you in the evening.
I love you in my dreams.

I love your voice,
your stories, your yawn,
your sleeping purr.

I love you.
Always have.
Always will.

I LOVE YOU BY HEART.

Unconditional love is rare. Cherish and savor it.
How lucky are we to love and be loved!

Take the time today to reach out and
share your love in some
unexpected way!

♥

PHR